BAREFOOT HELEN
AND THE
GIANTS

To Franny, who knows how to tell a story.
        ~ A.J.

For Eloise and Grace, two girls who could easily outwit
a giant or three!
        ~ K.B.

BAREFOOT HELEN AND THE GIANTS

by Andy Jones

Illustrated by Katie Brosnan

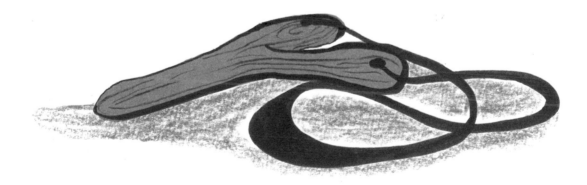

Chapter One

Once or twice upon a time or times, there was—or is, or isn't or wasn't, or wis or wisn't—an old couple, a fisherman and a fisherwoman, who to their great sorrow, have no children.

One evening while walking along a river path, they see a little girl wandering alone through the woods. Her hair is long and wild, and she wears clothes woven from birch bark, feathers, leaves, and grass. Although she speaks no human language, she is healthy, strong, and smart; she can climb the tallest tree and run as fast as light. She knows where all the animals live, where all the berries are, and how to sleep in a hollow tree or a deep cave.

At first the girl is shy and runs away, but the woman soon coaxes her from her hiding place by singing a sweet lullaby.

This wild girl is quite curious about the man and woman, and is soon sitting near them by the side of the river. Eventually she follows them home where she climbs up and sits on the supper table, and using her hands, gobbles up all the food the fisherwoman has laid out. Then she walks outside and falls asleep on the dog's cushion on the front bridge.

Do you know this girl?

The old couple do their very best to find the girl's mother and father. Messages are sent to all the neighbouring settlements; rewards are offered, town criers shout the story in the streets, but no one seems to know who she is.

That's it, then; the girl stays with them.

The fisherwoman and her husband love her and bring her up as their own. And they call her "Helen".

It's figured pretty generally Helen had been reared by black bears in the woods nearby. And that must be true because she is an ace salmon-fisher—she can put her hand in a waterfall, and with her sharp fingernails, hook a fish right out of the water, flip it in the air, catch it in her mouth, and swallow it in two gulps.

Helen soon learns to talk, to use a knife and fork, and *finally* to sleep indoors, but the fisherman and his wife can never get her to wear shoes. Her feet are very hairy, and no matter how icy the weather, they are never cold.

And strangely, she only has nine toes.

When she is ten years old, she starts working with her new mom and dad in the salt fishery. When she isn't fishing or salting codfish, she's happy to run barefoot in the bush, row boats with her friends in the harbour, go hunting, or have boil-ups on the beach.

This little family has no fancy clothes or fine furniture, but they have a good solid house with plenty of firewood, lots of vegetables in their root cellar, and fresh fish and game every day.

But then, one year, the fishing turns bad, and it stays bad for three years running. It seems as if the cod have disappeared forever.

So Helen says to her father, "Dad," she says, "we got to clear out of here—we got nothing left. We'll soon be starving. Come on we goes to live in the woods. I'll take care of the both of ye."

"No," says her father. "Your mother and I are too old for that. Tomorrow we'll move to the city. Pack your bags, girl."

So next morning they pack up. Now, all they have with them as they leave home is a billy-kettle, a handful of tea, a loaf of bread, a quarter pound of butter, and a jar of molasses. And it's over a day's walk to the city.

But luckily Helen has her slingshot with her—a powerful little stone launcher that can fit in the pocket of her dress.

Chapter Two

Helen and her mother and father walk and they walk and they keep on walking for hours and hours along the narrow wooded path to the city, until at lunchtime, they sit down by the side of a babbling brook, light a fire, boil the tea-kettle, and eat their bread, butter, and molasses. But as they're eating, her mom and dad can see that Helen has something on her mind. She stands up from the fire, walks over to the woods, and starts pacing back and forth, and back and forth, and back and forth.

Finally, her mother says, "Helly!" she says, "What's troubling you, maid?"

"Well," says Helen, "this is a hard thing to say, but I'm going to leave you."

"What?" says her mother, her heart missing a beat.

"Now, Mom, calm down," says Helen. "It's about time I went off to seek my fortune. And you know I could *never* live in a city. So I think I'll head off and settle somewhere in the forest. I'll be happy there."

"Heaven's sake, child, you can't do THAT!" her mom says. "You can't do that 'cause you'll be lost. We'll never see you no more!" And then she starts in bawling.

"Now, Mom," says Helen. "You know I'll come and visit."

"And ya got nothin' on yer feet … and ya only got nine toes."

"Mom!" says Helen. "Will ya forget about my feet?"

And then her mother says, "But ya got no grub. Come to the next town with us and get some food, now, Helly."

"No, no, no," says Helen, putting her hairy, four-toed foot down. "I'll be alright. I got my little sling, and I'll kill some game for to eat. Or I'll grab a salmon from the river."

"Whatever you want, my love," says her mother, trying her best to be brave.

Oh my, there's a very long and tearful parting. Sad indeed. For this was the first time Helen and her mother and father had been apart since she came to live with them.

Finally, Helen says goodbye and gives her mother the biggest kind of a bear hug and then she shakes hands with her old man—'cause that's the way it was in them days.

She leaves and they leave. She goes on and they go on.

Chapter Three

It's early afternoon; the sun is splitting the rocks and Helen is only down the path a couple of miles when she comes across a big beautiful blueberry patch, and

Helen. Loves. Blueberries.

—as much as life itself. She soon starts filling her face while wandering in circles among the berry bushes. When she's full to the brim and ready to explode from berries, she lies down for a little nap.

Three hours later, she wakes with a start to the sound of the biggest burp she's ever heard. BRRRRRUUUUUUURP! At first, she thinks it's her own burp—and that she's burped herself awake—but then she looks up and sees, far beyond the berry bushes, a big castle. She stands up, walks over, and peeks in through a hole in the castle door. There she sees three fearsome giants sitting at a kitchen table, laughing, and having a burping contest. They have just finished eating a flock of swans, three baby bears, and a barrel of gerbils. The giants are picking their teeth with telegraph poles.

Did you ever hear of **'GIANTS'?** Yeah? But these are not the friendly giants of *these* days, they're the cruel killer-giants of *them* days, and Helen has heard many stories about these very giants, how they have killed and eaten hundreds of people, and destroyed the homes and farms of many more.

The three giants are brothers, and their names are Bulleybummus, Arson-Puffin, and Dunch. Dunch is most particularly known for tearing up farmers' crops; Arson-Puffin for burning people's homes to the ground; and Bulleybummus for eating people in one gulp. His motto is *One chomp, no chew.*

And there they sit at the table, dressed in clothes that they themselves have clumsily stitched together out of hundreds of shirts, dresses, socks, coats, and trousers stolen from their poor dead victims!

Everyone wants to rid the kingdom of these gruesome creatures.

So, Helen comes up with a clever plan. She thinks to herself that she'll take her slingshot and bung a stone at Bulleybummus, who is sitting at the middle of the table with one brother at each end. She puts in a stone, hauls back, and fires right through the hole. It strikes the giant **—THWACKK!—**on the left side of his neck. The stone bounces off, but it stings the old brute.

Bulleybum roars at Arson-Puffin:
> "Beastly, beastly, be'est thee!
> Why didst thou fire at me?"

Arson-Puffin snaps back:
>Beastly be'est thee! T'warn't *me*.
>I didn't fire nothing at thee!

The big bully picks up a huge knife and bellows:
>"Yes, thou didst!
>>Fire again and lose thy life,
>>For I'll lop off yer head
>>With this girt big knife."

Helen snickers and fires another stone at him—**WHAMMO!** Well,
the old giant is in a rage. With no more ado, he takes the big knife
and he chops Arson-Puffin's head clean off.

Then Helen goes around to the other side of the castle,
finds another door with another hole, fires again, and strikes
Bulleybummus—**THWIK!**—as sharp as a needle on the right cheek.

The wicked old giant roars with pain, then turns
to his brother Dunch and yells:
>"Beastly, beastly, be'est thee!
>>Why did'st *thou* fire at me?
>>Shur, didn't I just lop off yother feller's head?
>>Hast thou a hankerin to end up dead?"

Dunch replies,
>"Beastly be'est *thee*! T'warn't me.
>I wouldn't fire nothing at thee!

Shur, when I sees thee, Bulley, my heart skips
I loves thee more than ripped-up parsnips"*

But the older giant cannot be budged, and he whispers fiercely
through his orange and yellow teeth:
      "Strike again and lose thy life
        For I'll level thy shoulders
        With this girt big knife!"

Helen lobs another stone and strikes him again!—**FWOKK!**

Well, the giant grabs the big knife and he chops Dunch's head off.

"Ohhh, that was alright," says Helen. "Now, that's two of 'em gone,
dead as dust."

Helen doesn't stop to think, but picks up another stone and lets fly
right into the giant's ear. That *really* stings, and the great Bulley lets
out a furious screech.
      "Beastly! Beastly! … uh, hey, hang on …"

"Uh, oh," says Helen …

Then this giantest of giants starts *thinking—for the first time in his life*.
In fact, he takes out a pen and paper and tries to figure it out with
Algebra! (The effort makes smoke pour out from his ears.)**
      "If there be … but three of we
        And two are gone, then that leaves me.

* *He has never actually tasted a sweet, delicious parsnip; he has only seen them torn up, gone*
  dunchy, and lying sadly in a farmer's field.
** *This smoke caused by friction from still new and unused thinking gears.*

If *x* is me and *c* is he
And *b* is he (the yother he)
And *c* and *b* are gone from me
Then there's got to be a '*d*'
In this equation here with me!

Oh, mercy me!
I'll squish this lowest common *d*
'Til he's a proper fraction of a flea!"

Oh, this giant is mad! He jumps up and he goes out through the door
looking for that lowest d, but Helen whips behind the door and hides.

Bulleybum starts sniffing around for the smell of human.
"Job to say where thou art now,
But I'll find thee anyhow.

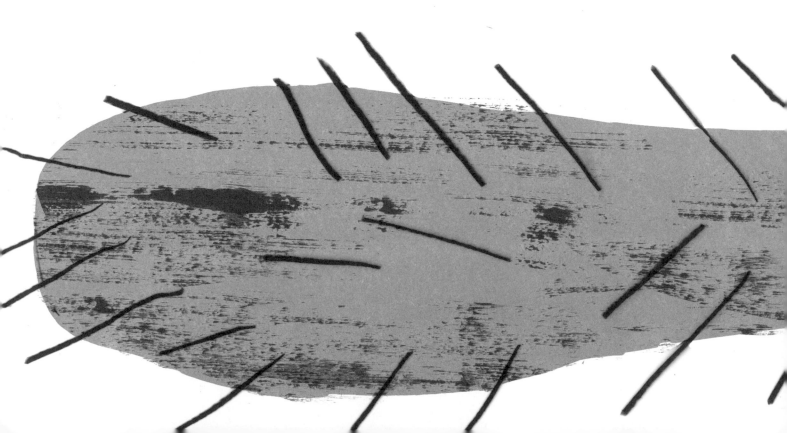

Since I've killed my own two brothers
Won't be hard to kill another!"

The giant looks all around but he can't see anyone. By an' by,
he hears **THUMPA, THUMPA, THUMPA, THUMPA!**

It's Helen's heart!

The giant smiles a wicked smile. Then he sees them—Helen's nine
hairy toes, sticking out from the under the door. He hauls the door
back, grabs Helen by the scruff of her neck, dangles her in the air,
and says in a terrifying whisper:
    "Come on in, hellion, whilst I kill thee.
    I can't tell thee how it thrills me—
    How I love to hear a puppy's cries
    'Fore I *whack* him 'tween the eyes."

He reaches for his killing bat …

Chapter Four

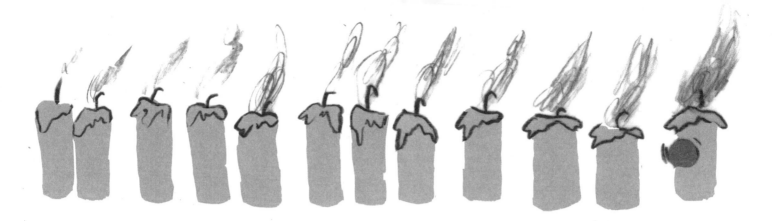

Now, Helen is trembling like a leaf, but somewhere down in the pit of her stomach, she finds her voice. "Hold on a bit, now. Hold on a bit, Mr. Giant," she says. "I got my little slingshot here, buddy. I can do a lot with this little weapon."

"**AIIIIIIIIIIRIGHT, Imp**" says the giant, forced to think once again.

> "I'll light twelve candles all in a line
> And if you dout *all twelve* it's fine.
> But, you only got *one shot*,
> And if one's still lit, then no matter what,
> I'll blend thee up (so's not to burp)
> Then, drink thee down with a mighty slurp!"

"What, only twelve candles? Ha! Pshaw! Pfuuff! That's easy," says Helen in her bravest voice. But her knees are knocking as loud as a bongo drum.

Then the giant says,
> "If thou art so keen …
> I'll make it **thirteen!**"

23

"Gotta learn to keep my mouth shut," says Helen under her breath.

Well, the giant lights the thirteen candles all abreast of one another. Helen goes to the other side of the room and her hands are shaking with fear, because her life depends on that *one shot*. Then, she takes a stone out of her pocket, puts it in the launcher, fires and **THIPTHIPTHIPTHIPTHIPTHIPTHIPTHIPTHIPTHIPTHIPTHIP!** ... she snuffs out *twelve* of the candles with the one stone.

But there's still one candle burning! Oh no ...

The giant's red eyes begin to glow with vile delight. He picks up his killing-bat ... but luckily a late summer squall blows in through that hole in the door and—**WHOOSHHH!**—puffs the last candle out.*

The giant is delighted! Helen is just the sharpshooter he is looking for.

He does a giant's happy-dance that shakes the ground for miles around. Then he says to her:
    "**AIIIIIIIIIIRIGHT, Insect**!!"

    "Thou made'st me kill my brothers two,
      For this I'm ever vexed at you!
      But, now I needs commit a slaughter
      So I can nab the king's young daughter
      And kill her outright—his precious honey—
      Unless he pays me bags of money!

* *Phew! Those little unexpected breezes are sometimes called 'fairy squalls.'*

But she's protected by a magic cat
(No, not the one who wears a hat).
That puss I've tried to kill these twenty years
With clubs and guns and swords and spears,
But now thy nimble sling wilt do the job
And turn that moggy into cat kebab!"

"Why are you such a scaredy cat about a pussy cat?" asks Helen.

The giant blushes. He looks about the room, afraid someone will over
hear him. Then he whispers:
"This little cat has a magic power;
Once she sees thee, friend, you'll surely cower,
'Cause she can swell up to a ten-foot lynx
Who'll chew thy brains out!
Then, once you're dead, she shrinks—
to a normal pussy once again,
Polite as catnip, right as rain."

"Gulp," says Helen. Then she starts bragging: "'Tis no trouble for me
to kill THAT cat. Why, you could steal that princess tonight if you want!"

"AIIIIIIIIIIRIGHT, Pipsqueak!!" says the giant.
"As soon as the midnight bell doth ring,
I and thou wilt visit the king,
And no one will suspect a single thing
For as thou knowst '**dead cats can't sing**!'"

And then the giant starts to laugh—
HAHAWHAWHAWHAWHAWHAW!
He laughs so loud that bricks fall out of the
chimney and plaster falls from the ceiling.
Bulleybummus is on the rampage!

For miles around people can
hear his laughter, and everyone
is terrified. Everyone, that is, except
the king's daughter herself, the Princess
Antoinette, who lays in bed and scoffs:
"Come ahead, Bulleybum. Ya don't scare
me, because we got a magic cat that's
just itching to lick out your brains
for breakfast!!!"

Then the princess starts to laugh
so loud it echoes off the hills and
through the kingdom—

HAWHAWHAWHAWHAWHAWHAW!
Slate shingles shake loose from the roof of the palace.

A cold shiver goes up Bulleybummus's back.

Chapter Five

And so, that night, at the chimes of midnight, Helen and the giant go to the palace, and guess what? There is a hole in the door there, too! They look through and see the sweet, innocent-looking, little pussy cat asleep on the table.

"Hah!" Helen whispers to the giant. "I can kill that cat in a wink."

But to tell the truth, Helen does not want to kill the cat, for

Helen. Loves. Cats.

—even more than she loves blueberries.

So, she puts her eye close to the door-hole, peers around the room, and sees an old clock with a pendulum—right over puss's head. Helen watches the pendulum going back and forth, and back and forth, and back and forth, and then she quietly says to the giant: "Just watch o' that pendulum!" and she fires the slingshot—***TZOOOM!***, hits the pendulum—***BTYANNG!***, and it comes down and strikes the cat on the head—**BOINNNG*!* ...

But it doesn't kill her, no. It just stuns her. (You know the expression "That stund cat"? Yeah? Well, that's where that expression comes from.)

The giant, now, he thinks the cat is dead and he's over the moon.

"**AlllllllllllRIGHT, Sparrow-fart!**" says the giant.

"Shhhh," says Helen.

"Sorry," says the giant, and then he whispers, "*AlllllllllllRIGHT, Sparrow-fart.*

"Slide like a serpent through all of the house—

Move smooth as a tiger, walk soft as a mouse.

Find Antoinette and give me a shout;

I'll climb up a ladder, then you hand her out."

Chapter Six

Well, Helen goes into the castle. She goes into every room and has a good gawk all around. By an' by she opens a door and there is the king in bed, sound asleep and holding a big sharp sword in his hand. He never goes to bed without that sword, in case the giants should ever get past the magic cat.

Very tenderly, Helen takes the sword out of the king's hand. "Harrumph!! Parrumph!! Gerbaphumph!!" says the king, beginning to wake up.

Helen doesn't know what to do. In her panic, she sings a lullaby to put the king back to sleep:
    "Hush now little king-a-ling
    The night bells go ding-a-ling
    The bad bee won't sting-a-ling
    As long as I sing-a-ling ...to *youuuuu.*"

It works! Soon the king is snoring like a brass band.

On up the stairs Helen goes, all the way to the attic, where covered in curtains and coats to fool the giants, Princess Antoinette sleeps in an old trunk.

Helen goes over to a little window and signals silently to the giant.

"*Alllllllllll*RIGHT, *Bunchberry!*" says the giant.

"Shhhh," says Helen.

"Sorry, Bunchberry," says the giant. Then, he whispers,

"I'll climb up faster than a drainpipe rat,

Then you hand me out the *Princess Dial!*"

The giant climbs up and up and up and up—all the way to the dormer window in the roof.

"Now," says Helen very softly, "poke your head right in through the window, buddy, because this princess weighs a ton. I know she looks small, but she's dense as lead. I can't lift her."

This doesn't make sense to Bulleybum. It just seems wrong—but he

Can't. Trust. His. Own. Brain.

At times like this he regrets never going to school. But, eager to kidnap the princess, he puts his head in through the window.

And what does he see? He sees Helen, standing there with a big smile on her face. The giant snarls at her, showing his orange and yellow teeth. He is waiting for Helen to say something.

"Knock, knock," whispers Helen.

"Who's there?" says the giant with a puzzled look.

"Russian sword," says Helen.

"Russian sword who?"

"Russian Sword Kutchaheadoff."

There is a long pause.

Bulleybummus is confused. "I don't get it," he grumbles.

"You will now," says Helen, and she takes the king's sword and … chops the giant's horrible head clean off—**SLOOSH!** The giant's head falls down in the room and his body falls down in the garden outside. The body makes a terrible **thuddddd**, but the princess is sleeping so soundly, and the king is snoring so loudly, no one wakes up.

Helen looks around the room. She sees Bulleybummus's head, still scowling from the knock-knock joke, lying on the floor. She sees the princess sound asleep in the trunk.

"What am I doing here?" Helen mutters to herself, "a big, poor, hairy-footed, nine-toed galoutte-girl holding a king's sword in a princess's bedroom … I gotta get back to the woods!"

So she takes a long last look at the snoring Antoinette, sneaks downstairs, drops the sword off in the snoring king's bedroom, passes the stunned and snoring pussy cat, and goes back to live in the woods *forever!*

And no one knows that Helen was the one who killed the giant.

 # Chapter Seven

The next morning, the king wakes up and goes downstairs.

The first thing he sees is the stunned cat. He thinks the cat is dead!

"Nobby!" he cries—that's the cat's name—"Nobby is dead! Oh no, if Nobby is dead, then the giant must have broke in last night! He must have got Antoinette!"

He starts wailing like a banshee, ringing every bell, and banging on every door as he runs up to the princess's room.

Meanwhile, his shouts awaken Antoinette who sees the giant's ghastly head on her floor. She just smiles and says, "Oh blessed day. You are finally dead, you wicked old buzzard. Let the joy-bells ring!

She's as happy as a dog with two tails.

The king comes into Antoinette's room. He is relieved to see that his daughter is alive and the dreadful giant is dead.

But where is the giant killer?

Nowhere to be seen.

"Now," says the king, "how are we going to find the brave giant killer? For that's one champion who'll get the keys to the kingdom."

"At the very least," says the princess.

So, they begin a search, and they search and they search and they search, high and low for ninety days. The searchers even ask directions from Helen as they crisscross the woods. Helen politely helps them find their way, but says nothing to anyone. She wants to live in peace in the bush—barefoot and free. She knows that no one gets the keys to the kingdom unless they wear shoes.*

'No shoes, no shirt, no keys' was a common phrase of the time.

Chapter Eight

But Princess Antoinette will not give up the search. She's as stubborn as a bed bug.

One day she says, "Father," she says, "I got an idea. Let's build an all-day all-night storytelling hotel. We'll put a sign out front saying *All you can eat. Nothing to pay. A yarn to spin.* And the giant-slayer is bound to come by and tell the story of how he or she or they did it."

"Good idea, Antoinette," says the king. "You, my ducky, are as smart as a whip."

"I know," says Antoinette.

And before you know it, she builds the storytelling hotel, and every night, it is blocked to the rafters with noisy crowds who speak every language in the world! There are sailors, waitresses, stonemasons, fishers, travelers, housemaids, clowns, tailors, seamstresses, shepherds, poets, bonesetters, midwives, nurses, nannies, wrestlers, hangashores, cooks, crooks, artists, and louts. There are people sleeping on daybeds, couches, Murphy beds, and fold-away lie-lows—stuffed into closets, pantries, porches, and balconies. Dresser drawers are removed as beds for babies; there are youngsters asleep in laundry baskets and grocery boxes, and on piles of coats.

These guests all have stories to tell—some are true, some are false—some are both. There are yarns about fairies, banshees, boo-darbies, demons, griffins, ghosts, tricksters, hags, and dragons. Singers sing their stories, dancers dance theirs. There are theatrical performances both tragical and comical; there are paintings on the walls, magic lantern shows, jokes, magic tricks, acrobatics, and riddles. Sometimes there is just free-form, unfocused laughter and tears, and, always and everywhere, there is an eternal mist of music, the lifeblood of any party, for fiddlers' hearts are ever in their bows and strings.

No one ever goes to bed until dawn. In fact, they call it the "Long Night Hotel."

Nobody guesses that the young, efficient maiden in a white bonnet who runs this good-time hotel is the Princess Antoinette.

The hotel is open for a whole year. Thousands of stories are told, but no one tells the one story Antoinette wants to hear.

Chapter Nine

One day, an old couple, a man and a woman, come to stay at the Long Night Hotel. The husband, Mose is his name, is a quiet man. But Lilly, his wife, is a walking storybook. Her first night she casts a spell as she spins yarns about cats paddling canoes, flying houses, fairy funerals, pretty fish, talking cakes, a woman without a face (!), legs made of gold, singing moose, dancing seals and the mouse who makes the world go round.

But as dawn breaks Lilly tells the best tale of all—a true story of how she and Mose got their daughter. It seems that they found the girl in the woods, that she had been brought up by bears, and that she still lives in the forest nearby.

The princess Antoinette is intrigued, and while Lilly is coming down off the stage, she asks Mose if she can meet their daughter.

"Yes, girl," he says. "We'll get her to come by. That's just what she needs, to make a friend in the neighbourhood—a fine young woman like yourself. What do you think, Lilly?"

"Go way, Mose," she says to her husband. "She won't go nowhere where she got to wear shoes."

"That's no odds," says Antoinette. "Tell her she can come as she is."

"Fair enough," says the old lady. "I'll ask her. But don't hold your breath."

The next day Lilly and Mose go to meet their daughter in the woods. (You must have guessed by now that they are Helen's mother and father.) The little family has a wonderful day together. Helen shows her mom and dad where all the animals live, where the berries are, the best fishing spots, her wonderful vegetable garden (with its giant green peas), her cabin that she's built into a cave in the side of a mountain, a tower she's made of pine trees, a swimming hole she's carved out of the rocks in the river, and a shrew, an otter, and a brown trout who come to visit her every day.

"Mom and Dad," says Helen, "why don't you move in here with me—there's lots o' heat and plenty to eat."

"So, you **are** lonely," says her father.

"Yes, b'y, a little," says Helen.

"Come to the city," says her mom. "You'll get used to it."

"No way," says Helen. "I couldn't breathe there."

"Well, Mose," says her mom. "Go on. Ask her."

"Ask me what?" says Helen.

"Will ya come and have supper with us at the Long Night Hotel tonight?" says her father.

"Oh, I spose," says Helen, "but I'll have to eat in the back yard, 'cause I'm not wearing shoes …"

"No. You can eat indoors," says Moses. "The young maid at the hotel says 'no shoes, no problem.' "

Chapter Ten

That night Helen goes to the hotel, where once again, her mother is the star of the evening. Her mom tells stories of Christmas dinner with the devil's grandmother, of building a fire out of truth and lies, of a princess who saves her seven brothers, and—once again— the story of the mouse who makes the world go round.

As the sun begins to rise, Antoinette turns to Helen.

"Can you tell a story yourself, maid?"

"No," says Helen. "Most times when they were telling stories in the kitchen, I was outside climbing trees."

"*In the dark?*" says Antoinette. "You were climbing trees in the dark?"

"Yup," says Helen. "If I don't scale ten trees after supper, ducky, I can't sleep!"

"That's true," says her dad.

"Then do you have any real-life adventures to report?" says the princess.

"Well," says Helen, looking around cautiously, "seeing as everyone else is gone to bed … I suppose I could tell you—if you promise not to tell anybody—how one time I … killed … some giants."

"What are you goin on about now?" says Helen's mother.

"Leave her be," says Mose.

The princess is frozen. She stands up. She stammers, "**G ... g ... giants** …,**"** she says. "Please, don't say another word 'til I get my father."

She runs out of the room.

"Oh my, oh my, oh my," says Helen's mother in a loud whisper. "You'll get us in trouble if you tell all the things you're after killin. Her father might be the game warden!"

The princess comes back into the room.

"Leave her alone now, Lilly," says Helen's father. "Let Helen tell her story."

This is the first time the princess hears the young woman's name. She lets the name sink in—then, with a faraway look, she says it aloud:

"Helen."

"Yes?" says Helen.

"Oh, ah, nothing" says the princess, blushing beet red, "tell your story … **Helen**."

"But the sun is up," says Helen's mother, worried that Helen might say the wrong thing, "and no one wants to hear *true* stories."

"Come on now, Lilly," says Helen's father, "give someone else the spotlight."

"Go way, Mose. I'm just thinkin that the young lady might like to go off to bed."

"I'm fine," says the princess, "and here comes my father. He'd love to hear the story."

"You're not the game warden?" says Lilly to the king.

"No, no," says the king. "I'm … the … janitor here at the hotel."

"Oh," she says, "I got to talk to you about the heat in our room …"

"Later, Lill," says her husband.

So, Helen starts her story.

Chapter Eleven

"Well, as Mother already told you in one of her stories, we ran into a spot of trouble last year and we headed out to the big city for to get jobs. And we were that poor, all we had left in the world was a billy-kettle, a loaf of bread, a jar of molasses, some butter, tea, and my trusty slingshot."

"True!" says Helen's mother. "Not a word of a lie."

Helen continues. "Now at midday we sat down to our little lunch by the side of a babbling brook—and perhaps it was the wrong occasion—but I decided to leave Mom and Dad, and set out on my own. I could *never* live in the city and … well there's something strange about my feet …"

"Yes, she only got nine toes, look!" says her mother, pointing at Helen's feet.

"Not *that*, Mother," says Helen. "The strange thing about my feet is that when I put shoes on them, I can't breathe. It's like my feet got lungs!"

"Fascinating … **Helen**," says the princess—who, I must tell you, gentle reader, if you believe in such things—is falling in love with Helen at this very moment. (Perhaps you saw it coming.)

"You never told us that, Helen," says her father.

"Well, there's lots I never told ye, and I suppose someday I will, but for now, listen while I tell how I met them giants."

"Yes, Mose, listen," says Helen's mother. "Let _her_ have the spotlight."

Helen smiles at Antoinette and continues.

"I told my parents I was leaving, gave a hug and a handshake, walked for about ten miles, had a big feed of blueberries and a nap. When I woke up I was in a dismal, withered garden—belonging to three terrible, murderous giants!"

"Bulleybummus, Arson-Puffin, and Dunch," say the princess and the king together.

"Exactly," says Helen.

"This is just the story we are looking for," says the princess.

"Well, it's not over yet," says Helen. "I crept up to a hole in the castle door, slung shots at Bulleybummus, and drove him into a fiendish temper. He blamed his two brothers and sliced their horrible heads clean off!"

"Oh, my!" says the princess, with a long, lingering look at Helen.

"Then, I fired one more time!" says Helen, looking sheepish.

"Oh, no …" says the princess.

"Oh, *yes,*" says Helen. "And even that dim-witted old giant was smart enough to see that it was *me* that whizzed that stone at him! Well, he was gonna eat me on the spot—*one chomp, no chew*—but I told him I was a good shot. To prove it he set up thirteen candles all in a row and I had to snuff 'em all with one stone from my slingshot. And guess what? I **did** it—," says Helen, boasting a bit and leaving out the *thirteenth* candle and the fairy squall.

"Of course ya did," says her mom, who is enjoying the story now.

"Then Bulleybummus tells me how truly, madly, and deeply he needs to *kidnap a princess* who is guarded by an enchanted cat."

"Nobby," says the princess.

"You know that cat?" says Helen.

"No, no, but … who hasn't heard of Nobby, the magical cat?" says the princess, telling lies.

"I never heard of him," says Helen's mother.

"Whatever," says Helen's father. "Keep talkin, Helen."

"Anyway, that night, at midnight, me and ol' Bulley sneak into the king's palace …"

"Sneakin into the king's palace?" says her mom. "I hope that's lies or you'll have us all in jail before the day is out."

"But first, the giant wants me to kill the cat," says Helen, "but

I. Love. Cats.

So instead, I hit the pendulum of the old clock, the pendulum falls down and—**ZONKO!** It stuns her. Doesn't kill her, just stuns her." *

"'Twas you that knocked out puss," says the king. "I thought the poor cat was dead!"

"Hush, Daddy," says the princess.

"Were you there?" asks Helen suspiciously.

"No, no," says the janitor-king, "but shur … everyone's heard what happened to Nobby, the royal cat."

"Hmmm," says Helen, "looks a lot like that cat right there."

She points to a cat sleeping by the hob of the fireplace.

"Oh, yes," says the king, "that's … Hobby, Nobby's brother."

"This is a *very* small kingdom," thinks Helen, as she continues with her story.

* As we already mentioned, this is the source of the expression "that stund cat".

"I went into the king's bedroom, nearly woke him up, sang him back to sleep, took the sword out of his hand, went up to the princess's bedroom, got the giant to climb a ladder, told him to poke his head in through the window, told him a knock-knock joke, chopped his head off with one slice, had a long look at the princess, the giant, and myself—and figured I'd best skedaddle."

"Oh," says the princess, "that's the story I wanted to hear. Oh, Father, I got the woman!"

Helen's mother panics. "What do you mean you 'got the woman.' What woman? What are ya talking about? Oh, you spoke too bold and now you're in trouble, Helen!"

Then she says to the king, "Are you the sheriff? If you are, you keep your hands off my girl or else ..."

"Lilly, Lilly, calm down," says Mose. "They seem happy enough with the story."

"Yes," says the king. "Calm down, Missus. I'll explain everything."

And he does.

And it's soon pretty obvious to everyone that Helen is going to get more than the keys to the kingdom.

Chapter Twelve

So the king and the princess call for a great celebration to honour Helen for her bravery. They declare *One Hundred and One Long Nights of Storytelling and Accordion Playing,* an outdoor festival that features stories by elders, children, teenagers, exotic dancers, eel fishers, throat singers, and choirs (there are more choirs than mice in this kingdom!). And every performance, by law, features an accordion player.

And strange to tell, there are reports of spirit storytellers who come back from the dead to tell tales and do recitations. Some of these ghosts had lived on these lands thousands of years ago. They take over the main stage in the early morning when the living storytellers are finished. There are always black bears in attendance.

Helen attends as many of the festival events as she is able, but mostly she spends her days and nights showing the Princess Antoinette around the bush.

On the one hundred and first night—the last night of the festival— Antoinette and Helen announce their intentions to settle down in the woods together. A great cheer goes up from the festival crowd.

Then Lilly, who's the emcee, announces the last performer of the festival: a surprise guest—an eel fisher by the name of Lucky Lucy. It seems she, too, has a true tale of Bulleybummus, Arson-Puffin, and Dunch.

"I'll make it brief," says Lucy. "That filthy family of fiendish giants murdered my dear husband, captured me, and told me I was to serve a stew for Arson-Puffin's birthday. A stew to be made out of our own little baby girl!"

The crowd gasps.

"And, I was to make the stew myself!"

The crowd gasps again.

"But I had a clever scheme. I cut off my daughter's little toe and put it in the stew pot …"

The crowd gasps a third time.

"… then I put five sheep and a flamingo into the stew, and hid my baby girl in a basket. When Bulleybummus tasted the stew, he said to me:
    'Baby stew? That's malarkey!
    What's in this pot, you sly young harpy?'

"And I rhymed him right back:
    'If this be not a stew-with-baby
    How come this toe is in the gravy?'

"Then I pulled the tiny toe out of the stew and showed it to Bulley-bum," says Lucy, "and the old ogre was happy enough. That night, when the giants went to sleep, I ran away with my baby. But the next day I came upon the hateful Dunch, who was tearing up a farmer's parsnip garden by the side of a river. He gave chase, and as I was running away, I tried to save my little darling by hiding her basket in a pretty patch of pitcher plants near a salmon pool. And that's the last I saw of my girl."

Mose, Helen's father, pipes up. "Were those pitcher plants near the salmon pool by Black Bear Caves?"

"They were," says Lucky Lucy.

"That's yer girl, there," says Mose, pointing to Helen. "And she's our girl, too. Now, look at her toes."

The whole crowd bursts into applause.

"Holey moley," says the princess to Helen. "It's your mother! Your real mother!"

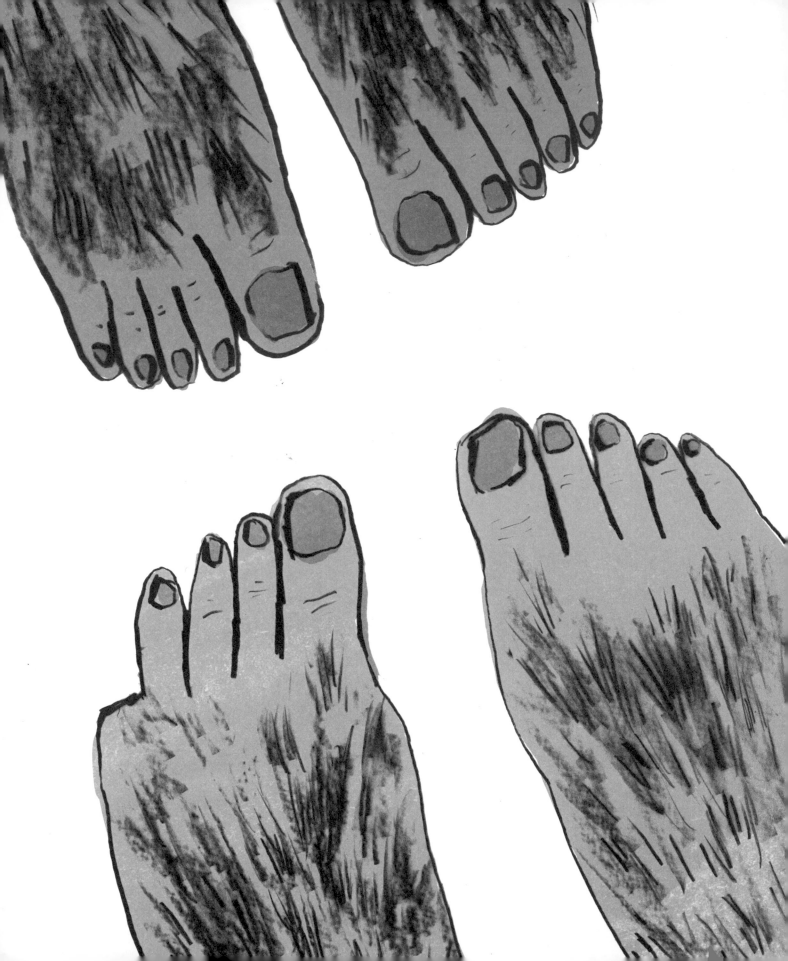

But then Lucy makes everyone hush up. "I'm sorry," she says, "but the toe I cut off was on the other foot."

The crowd groans with disappointment.

"Only kidding!" says Lucy. "That's my girl! There's no doubt about it ... shur, she's got my hairy feet!"

Lucky Lucy takes off her shoes and her own hairy feet are a match— except in number of toes.

"Lilly," says Lucy, "I'll gladly be a second mother to the girl."

"What more could a girl ask for than *two mothers*?" says Helen's mom.

Helen rolls her eyes ever so slightly.

Then there's a murmur in the crowd as a mama black bear walks up on to the stage. She looks lovingly at Helen.

"Actually it's *three mothers*," says Helen, hugging tight hold of the bear. "This is my bear mama who found me in the basket down by the pitcher plants. She brought me up as one of her cubs, then told me to follow Mose and Lilly back to their home. Do you want to hear *that* story?"

The crowd cheers.

And so, this story ends with the beginning of another story. And that story will end with another beginning, and thus we will story on, into the wormhole of time where we see Helen and Antoinette and their seven ten-toed children—who never wear shoes and live to this day in a tiny castle built into a cave—with two grandpas and three grandmas, and bears for uncles and aunts, and ghosts and trout and otters and shrews for friends—what you might call a *s'blendid family*.

And as Helen says to them all at the end of every day:

*From the poem "Human matters/ Humans matter" by Helen Bjarnansdottir

Notes about the story

Andy Jones's *Barefoot Helen and the Giants* was inspired by many versions of similar stories from Newfoundland and Labrador and from all over the world. The biggest influence was "Jack and the Three Giants" as told by Freeman Bennett of St. Paul's, Newfoundland, and published in Herbert Halpert and John Widdowson's seminal *Folktales of Newfoundland*.

Andy also studied "The Black Cat" as told by Angela Kerfont, which was collected by Marie-Annick Desplanques and published in *Folktales from Western Newfoundland*; "Jim Slowan" as told by John Roberts of Sally's Cove, and "The Black Chief of Slowan" as told by Freeman Bennett—both found in *Folktales of Newfoundland*; and "The Bear Maiden"—an Ojibwa folktale from Lac Courte Reservation, Wisconsin, USA, which was told in 1899 by Pä-skin´, an Ojibwa woman who was more than one hundred years old when the story was collected, and published in the *Journal of American Folklore* in 1902.

The catalyst for writing this book came from the play entitled *Jack-Five-Oh* by Andy Jones and Philip Dinn. It was written for the 50th anniversary of Newfoundland's joining the Canadian Confederation and includes a dramatization of "Jack and the Three Giants" which uses the 'storytelling hotel' as its basic structure. The play's co-writer, Philip Dinn (1949-2013) was a passionate Newfoundland folktale teller, a Jack believer, and a dedicated actor and musician in the Sheila's Brush Theatre Company's dramatized Jack tales series.

This book was also influenced by the many stories of Jack's giant-dispatching successes including "Jack and the Beanstalk"—in particular a Columbia Records 78 rpm recording from 1946 that was part of their *Let's Pretend series*.

As well, this book drew inspiration from "Mollie Whoopie", "The She Bear" (an Italian folktale), "Jack and His Stepdame", the Old Testament's "David and Goliath", and all the tales in *Little Jack and de Taxman*—Acadian stories told by Prince Edward Island's Antoinette Gallant.

Most of all this book exists because of a tall tale called *Marnie Parsons*.

ACKNOWLEDGEMENTS

Andy Jones would like to thank those who read various drafts of the text and gave him valuable feedback, including: Mary-Lynn Bernard, Marthe Bernard, Shannon Bramer, Marlene Creates, Megan Gail Coles, Mary Win Clair, Dermot Dawe, Lydia Derry, Camille Fouillard, Mark Ferguson, Alice Ferguson-O'Brien, Rob Finley, Susannah Polack-Finley, Peggy Hogan, Kelly Hickey, Darren Ivany, Robert Joy, Eleanor Blackmore Jones, Heather Logan, Don McKay, Frances Avalon McKeown, Jesse McKeown, Steven John Moore, Joanne Moore, Betty Jo Moore, Lucy Nichols, Will Nichols, Brenda O'Brien, Fiona Polack, Michelle Porter, Teya Rosenberg, Viv Seaward, Jamie Skidmore, Monique Tobin, Anne Marie Walling, and Andrea Schwenke-Wylie.

Special thanks to Eleanor Blackmore Jones for her editorial advice, ideas, and suggestions; to Darren Ivany for his ongoing research, administrative, and organizational help; and to Memorial University's Queen Elizabeth II Library for providing a warm, well lit, and quiet working space, as well as access to their incredible collection of folktale books.

The king's lullaby was inspired by "The Bells of Hell Go Ting-a-ling-a-ling" a popular Salvation Army hymn and a British airmen's song from World War I.

Andy Jones also thanks singer, folklorist, and friend Anita Best.

This book was designed by Veselina Tomova of Vis-à-vis Graphics, St. John's, NL,
and printed in Canada.

978-1-927917299

Running the Goat, Books & Broadsides is grateful to Newfoundland and Labrador's Department
of Tourism, Culture, Industry, and Innovation for support of its publishing activities
through the province's Publishers Assistance Program, the Canadian Department of Heritage
and Multiculturalism for support through the Canada Book Fund,
and the Canada Council for the Arts for support
through its Literary Publishing Projects program.

Newfoundland
Labrador

Canada Council   Conseil des arts
for the Arts   du Canada

Funded by the Government of Canada
Financé par le gouvernement du Canada   Canadä

Running the Goat
Books & Broadsides Inc.
General Delivery/54 Cove Road
Tors Cove, Newfoundland and Labrador A0A 4A0
www.runningthegoat.com